Carin Berger

Finding Spring

Greenwillow Books
An Imprint of HarperCollinsPublishers

The forest was growing cold.

Mama said that soon it would be time to sleep,

but all Maurice could think about was his first spring.

"S-p-r-i-n-g! Spr-ing! SPRING!" he sang as they filled up on berries.

"I wish it was spring right now," Maurice told Mama.

"Waiting is hard," she said. "Right now it is time to sleep."

"Maybe you will dream about spring,"
Mama whispered.

Soon she was softly snoring,

but Maurice was wide awake.

"I will go find spring!" he said.

And
off
he
went.

Everyone in the forest
was busy.

"I am looking for spring,"
Maurice told Squirrel.
"That might take a while,"
Squirrel chittered,
turning to bury
a large acorn.

"I am looking for spring,"
he told Rabbit.
"Not yet!" Rabbit giggled
before dashing into
his warm burrow.

Deer didn't even look up
from her grass.

"I am looking for spring,"
he told Robin.
"Everything in its time,"
Robin said.
Then she flew south.

The woods
smelled musky,
and there was
something new
and tangy
in the air.

"I smell spring!"
said Maurice,
as he hurried
along.

Suddenly, Maurice felt an icy sting on his nose. "Is that spring?" he asked.

A beautiful crystal landed on his paw. "Spring?"

The crystal disappeared,
but soon there was another.
And another. And another!
Maurice chased after them.
Spring was hard to catch!

He chased them . . .

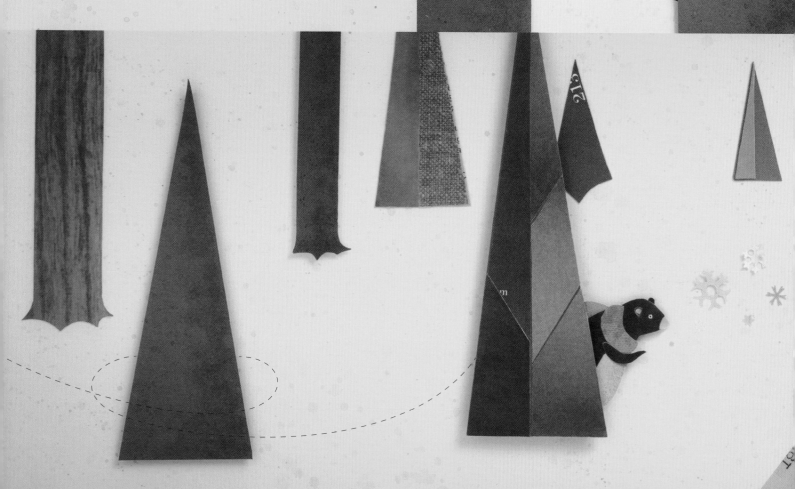

past dry leaves,

past bare branches,

over the frozen stream . . .

all the way to the Great Hill,

"W O W!" said Maurice.

"S-p-r-i-n-g! Spr-ing!
I FOUND SPRING!"
he sang, as he scooped up
a bit to take home.

Back in the den, Maurice snuggled happily against Mama.

He slept and slept and slept.

When he woke up,
everyone had already
gathered in the meadow.
"I brought you some spring,"
Maurice announced.

But spring was gone.

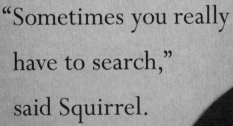

"Where *is* it?" he asked.
"Spring can be hard to
find," said Robin.
"Maybe it's hiding."
Rabbit giggled.
Deer just blinked.
"Sometimes you really
have to search,"
said Squirrel.

"Let's look again," Mama said.

So Maurice led them back through the forest.

He saw blooming branches.

And bright green buds.

He saw the rushing stream.
Everything had changed,
and Maurice knew just what to do.

"To the Great Hill!" he cried.

And at last, there it was.

Maurice had finally found S P R I N G!

In memory of David Rakoff.
With love.

With gratitude for the photography by Porter Gillespie.

Finding Spring. Copyright © 2015 by Carin Berger. All rights reserved. Manufactured in China. For information address HarperCollins Children's Books, a division of HarperCollins Publishers, 195 Broadway, New York, NY 10007. www.harpercollinschildrens.com. The illustrations in this book are assemblages created using a combination of cut paper and found ephemera. Each piece was then photographed digitally to prepare the full-color art. Photography by Porter Gillespie. The text type is 22-point Perpetua. Library of Congress Cataloging-in-Publication Data. Berger, Carin, author, illustrator. Finding spring / Carin Berger. pages cm "Greenwillow Books." Summary: Too excited to hibernate through his first winter, a bear cub tries to find spring. ISBN 978-0-06-225019-3 (hardcover) [1. Spring—Fiction. 2. Winter—Fiction. 3. Seasons—Fiction. 4. Bears—Fiction.] I. Title. PZ7.B45134Fi 2015 [E]—dc23 2014003155 14 15 16 17 18 SCP 10 9 8 7 6 5 4 3 2 1 First Edition

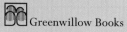 Greenwillow Books